Sadie's Snowy Tu B'Shevat

For Elaine Barenblat, whose whimsical creativity and dedication inspire me daily. —J.K.

For my mother with love. —J.F.

Text copyright © 2018 by Jamie Korngold
Illustrations copyright © 2018 by Julie Fortenberry

KAR-BEN PUBLISHING, INC.
An imprint of Lerner Publishing Group, Inc.
241 First Avenue North
Minneapolis, MN 55401 USA
1-800-4-KARBEN
Website address: www.karben.com

Library of Congress Cataloging-in-Publication Data

The Cataloging-in-Publication Data for *Sadie's Snowy Tu B'Shevat* is on file at the Library of Congress.
ISBN 978-1-5124-2677-9 (lib. bdg.)
ISBN 978-1-5124-2679-3 (pbk.)
ISBN 978-1-5124-9846-2 (EB pdf)

LC record available at https://lccn.loc.gov/2016059660

Manufactured in China
2-51011-23346-5/24/2021

0122/B1155/A4

Sadie's Snowy Tu B'Shevat

By Jamie Korngold

illustrated by Julie Fortenberry

KAR-BEN
PUBLISHING

It was Tu B'Shevat, the birthday of the trees,
and Sadie was ready to celebrate by planting a tree.

She took her Tu B'Shevat book off the shelf.

She read, "All you need is a shovel."
Sadie grabbed a shovel.

She read, "And a special spot."
Sadie thought about the best
spot to plant a new tree.

The spot would need lots of sunshine so that the
tree would grow tall enough to hold a swing.

The spot would need lots of room so that the tree would grow branches for climbing.

The spot would need lots of rich soil so that the tree would grow crunchy, sweet apples.

Sadie picked a spot.

She read, "Now dig a deep hole."

Sadie dug.

And dug.

And dug.

And dug.

And dug.

She read, "Now plant a young sapling."

Sadie went inside. "Mama, can you help me plant a tree?" she asked.

"Sweetheart, that won't work," said her mother. "You can't plant a tree in the middle of winter. It will freeze."

So Sadie asked Daddy for help.

"It won't work," said Daddy.
"You can't plant a tree in the snow.
It can't live."

Sadie asked Grandpa for help. "It won't work, honey," said Grandpa. "You can't plant a tree when it's cold. Its roots won't be able to grow."

Finally, Sadie asked Ori for help.
"I'll help you plant a tree," said Ori

. . . And he did.

Grandma brought them hot chocolate to drink under the tree.

"Happy Tu B'Shevat," they sang.

"Grandma," asked Sadie, "if Tu B'Shevat is the holiday when we're supposed to plant trees, why is it in winter when we can't plant trees?"

"In Israel, where the holiday was created," explained Grandma, "it is spring—the perfect time for tree planting!"

"When I was a little girl, we planted parsley on Tu B'Shevat instead of trees. We put parsley seeds in pots on the windowsill."

"We watered them every day and watched them grow.
They looked like miniature trees."

"Then, on Passover, we picked the parsley to dip in salt water at our seder."

"That's a great idea!" said Sadie. "Let's do it!"

Sadie, Ori, and Grandma went inside.

Sadie said, "All you need is a shovel!" They each grabbed a spoon.

Grandma said, "And seeds for planting!"
And they each planted their parsley seeds.

Ori said, "And a special spot!" They each picked a spot on the windowsill. **"Happy Tu B'Shevat!"** sang Sadie and Ori.

And two months later . . .
"**Happy Passover!**" sang Sadie and Ori.

Tu B'Shevat, the 15th day of the Hebrew month of Shevat, is the Jewish new year for trees. While it is winter in much of the world, in Israel the almond trees are beginning to bloom, announcing the start of spring. People celebrate the holiday by planting new trees, but in places where it is too cold to plant, families celebrate by eating fruits that grow in Israel such as almonds, oranges, figs, dates, and carob.

Rabbi Jamie S. Korngold received ordination from the Hebrew Union College-Jewish Institute of Religion and is the founder and spiritual leader of the Adventure Rabbi Program.
She lives in Boulder, Colorado.

Julie Fortenberry is an abstract painter and a children's book illustrator.
She has a Master of Fine Arts from Hunter College in
New York and lives in Philadelphia.